DREAMWORKS

RISE OF THE GUARDIANS

JAMIE
TO THE RESCUE!

adapted by Tina Gallo
illustrated by Zack Franzen and Charles Grosvener

Ready-to-Read

Simon Spotlight

New York   London   Toronto   Sydney   New Delhi

SIMON SPOTLIGHT
An imprint of Simon & Schuster Children's Publishing Division
1230 Avenue of the Americas, New York, New York 10020
Rise of the Guardians © 2012 DreamWorks Animation L.L.C.
All rights reserved, including the right of reproduction in whole or in part in any form.
SIMON SPOTLIGHT, READY-TO-READ, and colophon are registered trademarks of Simon & Schuster, Inc.
For information about special discounts for bulk purchases, please contact Simon & Schuster Special Sales at
1-866-506-1949 or business@simonandschuster.com.
Manufactured in the United States of America 0812 LAK
First Edition
2 4 6 8 10 9 7 5 3 1
ISBN 978-1-4424-5259-6 (pbk)
ISBN 978-1-4424-5260-2 (hc)
ISBN 978-1-4424-5262-6 (eBook)

Jamie Bennett loves reading stories about mysteries and the unexplained. Little does he know that his ordinary life is about to become extraordinary!

On his walk home from school one day, a snowball hits Jamie right in the back of his head. *POW!*
When he turns around, there isn't anyone near him.
Which of his friends threw it?
Where did it come from?

What Jamie doesn't know is that
Jack Frost threw it. Jamie can't see
Jack Frost . . . yet.

It doesn't really matter who started the fight. Now it is an all-out war! No matter how fast Jamie throws his snowballs, he never seems to run out. It's the best snowball fight ever!

Jack Frost leads the way as Jamie
and his friends slide down a hill.
He blasts a path of ice behind him.
It's very slippery. . . .

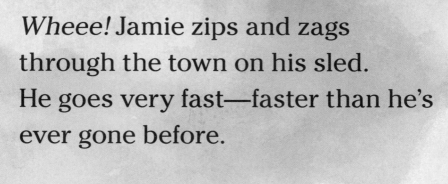

Wheee! Jamie zips and zags through the town on his sled. He goes very fast—faster than he's ever gone before.

He doesn't see that Jack Frost
is with him the entire way.

Jack Frost creates a huge ice ramp.
It launches Jamie up and over the
statue in the center of town.
Jamie loves every minute of the ride!

When Jamie's sled finally lands, his friends gather around him, and ask if he's okay.
Jamie smiles and holds up a tooth! That means the tooth fairy is coming!

That night, while Jamie is asleep, Jack Frost and Tooth come to his bedroom to collect his lost tooth and leave a coin.

But while Tooth is taking Jamie's
tooth, the other Guardians burst
through Jamie's window!
Tonight, the Guardians are helping
Tooth collect teeth because Pitch,
the Boogeyman, has captured
her Mini Fairies!

Jamie wakes up and shines a
flashlight at the foot of his bed.
He is surrounded by Guardians!

Jamie is thrilled to see them.
He has so many questions!

But Jamie must go back to sleep. Sandy tosses his dreamsand at Jamie, but it accidentally hits the Guardians and they all fall asleep!

Jamie laughs at the sight of North, Bunny, and Tooth sound asleep on his floor.
Sandy sprinkles dreamsand directly on Jamie, and soon he is asleep too.

On Easter Sunday, Jamie searches
for Easter eggs.
He is excited to see what goodies
Bunny delivered.
But he can't find anything.

Jamie wonders what has
happened to Bunny.
He's sure it wasn't a dream
when he saw the Guardians
by his bed.

Later that night, Jamie is alone in his room. He is talking to his favorite stuffed rabbit. He says he needs proof in order to keep believing.

Jack Frost has been listening outside
of Jamie's window. He wants Jamie
to believe! He ices the window, and
then draws a picture of an Easter egg
and a rabbit.

Jamie can see Jack now.
Jack is so excited that he makes it
snow in Jamie's room!

Jamie keeps believing in
the Guardians!

The Guardians return to Jamie's town. Jamie learns that Pitch and his Nightmares have made children stop believing. He is the last child who still believes in the Guardians and they need his help.

Pitch tries to frighten Jamie. But Jamie stands up to Pitch. "I believe in you," he says. "I'm just not afraid of you."

Jamie and Jack start
a snowball fight with Pitch!
Jamie discovers that when his
snowballs hit the Nightmares, they
turn into golden dreamsand!

Jamie and Jack wake up Jamie's friends.
Jack makes it snow in their rooms too!
They all run outside and join in a
snowball fight against Pitch.
No one is afraid of him anymore.

Dreamsand swirls through the
town, turning everyone's nightmares
back into beautiful dreams.

The Guardians thank Jamie for helping
them defeat Pitch. Jamie asks Jack if he
will ever see him again. Jack tells Jamie
that the Guardians will always be in
his heart—which kind of makes him a
Guardian too.